Pocahontas

Picture words

Pocahontas

Powhatan

John Smith

Chief

tribe

Ladybird  Readers

Pocahontas

Series Editor: Sorrel Pitts
Text adapted by Nicole Irving
Activities written by Catrin Morris
Illustrated by Abdi

LADYBIRD BOOKS

UK | USA | Canada | Ireland | Australia
India | New Zealand | South Africa

Ladybird Books is part of the Penguin Random House group of companies
whose addresses can be found at global.penguinrandomhouse.com.
www.penguin.co.uk   www.puffin.co.uk   www.ladybird.co.uk

Penguin
Random House
UK

First published 2020
001

Printed in China

A CIP catalogue record for this book is available from the British Library

ISBN: 978-0-241-40175-0

All correspondence to:
Ladybird Books
Penguin Random House Children's
80 Strand, London WC2R 0RL

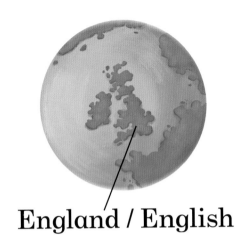

England / English

forest

vegetables

rich

gun

prison

Pocahontas was a happy girl. She loved the forests, the rivers, and all the animals near her home.

Pocahontas was the daughter of Powhatan.

Powhatan was Chief of the tribe.

Powhatan's tribe lived in a fine place. They got fruit and vegetables from their farms.

They got meat from the animals in the forests, and fish from the rivers and sea.

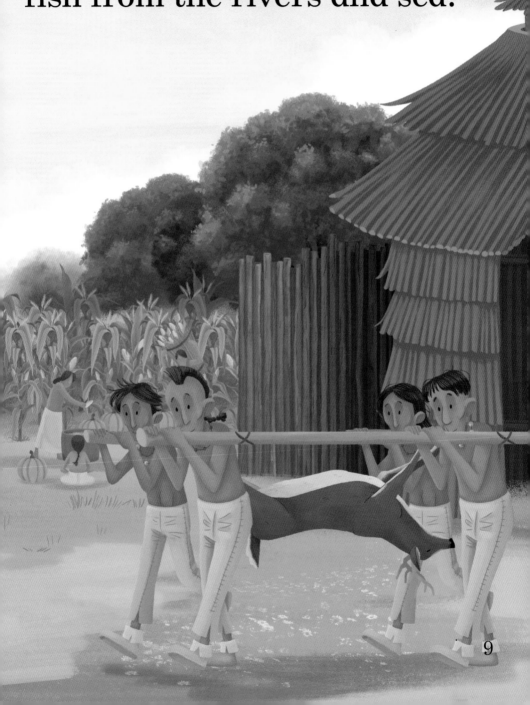

Then, English men
came in big boats.
They crossed the sea from
their country, England.

"We can live here, and carry fine things to England on our boats," the English men thought. "We can sell them there and get rich."

"Look," said the people in the tribe. "It's winter now. The English men want our food."

The English men had guns.
The tribe was not safe.

One day, some people from Powhatan's tribe caught an English man.

They took him to Powhatan.

"My name is John Smith,"
said the man. "I am
your friend."

"Put him in prison!"
Powhatan said.

John stayed in prison for many days. Powhatan's family gave him food.

Powhatan thought a lot about the English man. One day, he said, "Bring John here."

The men in Powhatan's tribe
wanted to kill John, but
Pocahontas remembered the
English men's guns.

She ran to John. "We mustn't kill him," she said.

Powhatan remembered the English men's guns, too. "My daughter is right," he thought.

"Go," he told John.

John went back to the town. He and Pocahontas were friends now. She taught John words in her language, and he taught Pocahontas English.

Soon people talked about them. "Pocahontas loves John," they said, "and he loves her."

"Pocahontas helped Powhatan's tribe and the English people to be friends," they said.

People liked
Pocahontas' story,
and she was
soon famous.

Activities

The key below describes the skills practiced in each activity.

Spelling and writing

Reading

Speaking

Critical thinking

Preparation for the Cambridge Young Learners exams

1 Look and read. Choose the correct words and write them on the lines.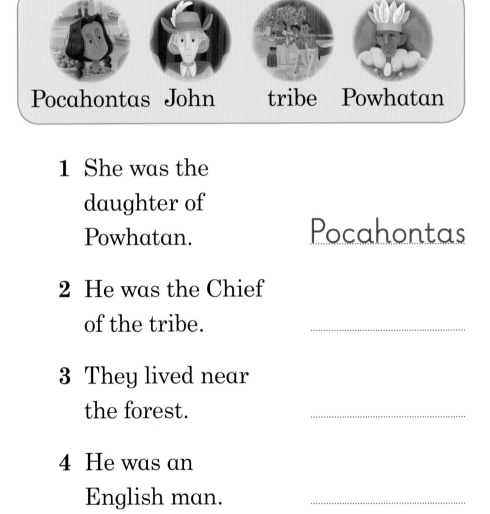

Pocahontas   John   tribe   Powhatan

1 She was the daughter of Powhatan.

Pocahontas

2 He was the Chief of the tribe.

3 They lived near the forest.

4 He was an English man.

2 Circle the correct words.

Pocahontas was a happy girl. She loved the forests, the rivers, and all the animals near her home.

Pocahontas was the daughter of Powhatan.

Powhatan was Chief of the tribe.

1 **Pocahontas** / **Powhatan** was a happy girl.

2 She loved the **forests,** / **vegetables,** the rivers, and all the animals near her home.

3 Pocahontas was the **mother** / **daughter** of Powhatan.

4 Powhatan was Chief of the **tribe.** / **English men.**

3 Match the words to the pictures.

1 Chief

2 forest

3 gun

4 prison

5 rich

6 vegetables

a

b

c

d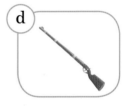

e

f

4 Look and read. Put a ✓ or a ✗ in the boxes. 📖 ✿

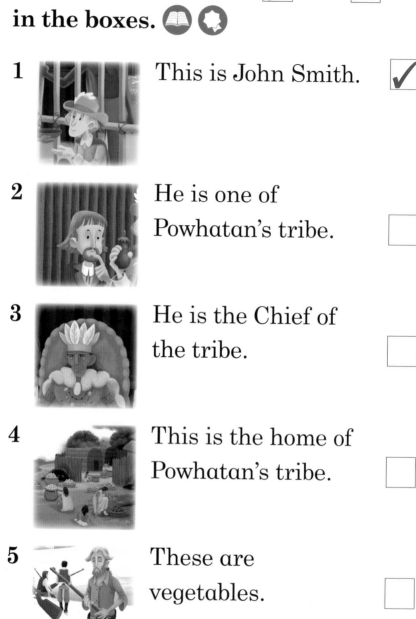

1   This is John Smith.   ✓

2   He is one of Powhatan's tribe.   ☐

3   He is the Chief of the tribe.   ☐

4   This is the home of Powhatan's tribe.   ☐

5   These are vegetables.   ☐

5 Write the missing letters.

gl   ie   is   re   ta

1    E n g _g_ _l_ a n d

2    C h _____ _____ f

3    f o _____ _____ s t

4    v e g e _____ _____ b l e s

5    p r _____ _____ o n

6 Circle the correct pictures.

1 Pocahontas lived there.

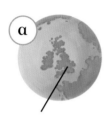  

2 People listened to him.

3 The English men had these.

4 The tribe was not safe.

  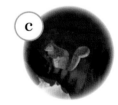

7 **Complete the sentences.**
Write a—d.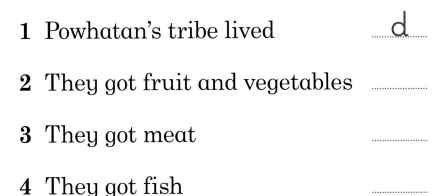

1 Powhatan's tribe lived ....d........

2 They got fruit and vegetables ....

3 They got meat ....

4 They got fish ....

a from the animals in the forests.

b from their farms.

c from the rivers and sea.

d in a fine place.

8 **Ask and answer the questions with a friend.** 💬

"We can live here, and carry fine things to England on our boats," the English men thought. "We can sell them there and get rich."

1 Who are these people?

They are English men.

2 Where are they?

They are . . .

3 What do they want to do?

They want to . . .

9 Look and read. Write the correct words in the boxes. 📖 ✏️ ❓

boats   fish   guns

meat   hats   vegetables

What Powhatan's tribe had	What the English men had
	boats

10 **Read the story. Write some words to complete the sentences.**

"Look," said the people in the tribe. "It's winter now. The English men want our food."

The English men had guns. The tribe was not safe.

1 It was .... *winter* .... then.

2 The .... men wanted the tribe's food.

3 They had ...., and the tribe was not safe.

11 Circle the correct sentences.

1

    a The tribe caught an animal.

    b The tribe caught an English man.

2

    a They took him to England.

    b They took him to Powhatan.

3

    a John went to prison.

    b John went to the forest.

4

    a Powhatan's family gave John food.

    b Powhatan's family gave John clothes.

12 Write the correct verbs.

John stayed in prison for many days. Powhatan's family gave him food.

Powhatan thought a lot about the English man. One day, he said, "Bring John here."

1 John **(stay)** ⟶ stayed ⟶ in prison for many days.

2 Powhatan's family **(give)** .... him food.

3 Powhatan **(think)** .... a lot about the English man.

4 One day, he **(say)** ...., "Bring John here."

5 The men in Powhatan's tribe **(want)** .... to kill John.

13 Circle the correct answers.

1 What did Pocahontas remember?
   a The English men's boats.
   b The English men's guns.

2 Did the men in the tribe kill John Smith?
   a Yes, they did.
   b No, they didn't.

3 What did Pocahontas want?
   a She wanted the English men and Powhatan's tribe to be friends.
   b She wanted the English men to go.

14 Who said this?

the English men

Powhatan

the tribe

John Smith

1 "We can live here," said
<u>the English men</u>.

2 "It's winter now. The English men want our food," said the people in

....

3 "I am your friend," said

....

4 "Put him in prison!" said

....

Write *safe*, *rich*, *happy*, *fine*, or *big*.

1 Pocahontas was a
......happy...... girl.

2 Powhatan's tribe lived in a
.... place.

3 Then English men came in
.... boats.

4 "We can sell their fine things
and get ...."

5 The English men had
guns. The tribe was not
....

16 Order the story. Write 1—4.

.... Pocahontas helped Powhatan's tribe and the English people to be friends.

......1...... Powhatan's tribe lived in a fine place and were happy.

.... The English men came and wanted to take their fine things.

.... The men in Powhatan's tribe caught John Smith and put him in prison.

17 **Ask and answer the questions with a friend.**

1

> *Do you live in a village, a small town, or a big city?*

> *I live in a big city.*

2 Do you like it there?
Why? / Why not?

3 Are there forests and rivers near your home?

Ladybird 🐞 Readers

Visit www.ladybirdeducation.co.uk
for more FREE Ladybird Readers resources

- ✓ Digital edition of every title*
- ✓ Audio tracks (US/UK)
- ✓ Answer keys
- ✓ Lesson plans

- ✓ Role-plays
- ✓ Classroom display material
- ✓ Flashcards
- ✓ User guides

Register and sign up to the newsletter to receive your FREE classroom resource pack!

*Ladybird Readers series only. Not applicable to *Peppa Pig* books.
Digital versions of Ladybird Readers books available once book has been purchased.